This book
belongs to:

NIKKI

MESSAGE TO PARENTS

This book is perfect for parents and children to read aloud together. First read the story to your child. When you read it again, run your finger under each line, stopping at each picture for your child to "read." Help your child to figure out the picture. If your child makes a mistake, be encouraging as you say the right word. Point out the written word beneath each picture in the margin on the page. Soon your child will be "reading" aloud with you, and at the same time learning the symbols that stand for words.

Library of Congress Cataloging-in-Publication Data

Meltzer, Lisa.
  The elephant's child / retold by Lisa Meltzer ; illustrated by Pat Stewart.
    p. cm. — (A Read along with me book)
  Summary: A rebus version of the Rudyard Kipling story that tells how elephants got their long trunks.
  ISBN 0-02-898238-X
  [1. Elephants—Fiction. 2. Rebuses.] I. Stewart, Pat Ronson, ill. II. Kipling, Rudyard, 1865–1936. The elephant's child.
III. Title. IV. Series.
PZ7.M51648E1   1989
[E]—dc19   89-631
                                                        CIP
                                                        AC

The Elephant's Child

A Read Along With Me Book

Retold by **Lisa Meltzer**
Illustrated by **Pat Stewart**

CHECKERBOARD PRESS
NEW YORK

Long ago in Africa, did not

have trunks. They had only big

bulgy noses that could wriggle. At

that time there was **1** little

child who asked ever so many

questions.

He asked the why her

feathers grew just so. He asked the

 why he had spots. So the

 and the spanked him.

He asked the why her eyes

were red, and the spanked him.

But still the child asked

questions! He asked about

everything he saw, or heard, or

felt, or smelled. And everyone

spanked the child.

ostrich

giraffe

hippo

one

elephant

crocodile

animals

 day the child asked,

"What does the eat for dinner?"

"HUSH!" said all the . And they

spanked him for a very long time.

Now, the child had never

seen or heard or felt or smelled or

touched a . All he knew was

that the lived by the .

"I will go to the to ask what

the eats for dinner," he said.

"Good-bye," said all the ,

and they spanked the child

one more time for good luck.

The child traveled for

days. At last he came to the

jungle. There he met a . It

was coiled around a .

river

three

snake

tree

crocodile

elephant

snake

"Can you please tell me what

the eats for dinner?" asked

the child.

"What?" said the . And

the spanked the little

child.

The child did not like being

spanked. So he said good-bye to

the and he walked to the

 . There he stepped on a log

of wood. But it was really the !

"Have you seen a in these

parts?" asked the child.

The lifted his tail out of the

 . The child stepped

back. He did not want to be

spanked.

river

"Come here, little child," said the . "I am the ."

"Why, you are the very animal I am looking for," said the child.

"Can you please tell me what you eat for dinner?"

"Come closer," said the . "I will whisper the answer to you."

So the child put his head close to the musky, tusky mouth of the .

elephant

crocodile

"I think," said the , "today I will begin with child!" And he caught the child by his nose and pulled. The child was very surprised. Poor child! His nose began to stretch and stretch. This hurt more than a spanking!

snake

tree

elephant

one

The scuffled down from the . He knotted himself around the child. "Pull, little child!" said the . The child and the pulled 1 way and the pulled the other way.

Poor child! His nose stretched

and stretched into a . With a

loud POP the let go.

The child fell back. "Thank

you," he said to the . Then

he hung his poor stretched

in the to cool and shrink.

After days, the was

cool. But it was still long. It was a

real just like have today.

crocodile

trunk

elephant

river

three

elephants

fly

elephant

river

trunk

snake

By and by a landed on the child and stung him. The child lifted his trunk out of the and hit the .

"You could not have done that with your old ," said the .

"You are right," said the child. Then he started for home.

Across Africa he went, frisking and whisking his . He learned to do all kinds of things with it. He

cooled his head with a schloop of

mud. He sang a little song.

At last the child arrived

home. The were glad to see

him. "How do you do?" said the

 child.

animals

animals

elephant

one

elephants

"Come here and be spanked for asking," the said.

"Pooh," said the child. "You know nothing about spanking, but I do." Then he knocked over **1** of his brother .

"Oh, bananas!" they said. "What

have you done to your nose?"

"I got a new from the

who lives in the ," said the

 child. "I asked him what he

eats for dinner, and he gave me this."

trunk

crocodile

river

animals

elephant

monkey

elephants

river

crocodile

"It is very ugly," said the .

"But it is very useful," said the child, and he picked up the and threw him into a beehive.

Then that bad child spanked all the for a long time. Finally all the hurried off to the to get new noses from the . When they came back, nobody spanked anybody anymore. And ever since that

Words I can read

- ☐ animals
- ☐ crocodile
- ☐ elephant
- ☐ elephants
- ☐ fly
- ☐ giraffe
- ☐ hippo
- ☐ monkey

- ☐ one
- ☐ ostrich
- ☐ river
- ☐ snake
- ☐ three
- ☐ tree
- ☐ trunk

day, all the you will ever see,

and all those that you will not,

have trunks just like the trunk of

the little child.

elephants